MW01247969

Sleep Stories

A Collection of Short Stories

Amber Holster

Sleep Stories
A Collection of Short Stories

Copyright © 2023 by Amber Holster

Paperback ISBN: 978-1-63812-824-3
Ebook ISBN: 978-1-63812-825-0

Published by Paper Leaf Agency   07/17/2023

Paper Leaf Agency
888-208-0170
admin@paperleafagency.com

SLEEP STORIES

A Collection of Short Stories

IN LOVING MEMORY OF
GRANDMA IDA

INTRODUCTION

This is a small collection of short stories that came to me in my dreams. I thought it would be fun to incorporate them all together and try and make them more fluid. I purposely picked these types of dreams because I thought they could be kind of creepy and interesting. I also thought writing something like this would be really fun for me. This isn't a normal introduction as it doesn't really introduce the story but, more or less introduce the kind of mindset I was in while writing these stories. This left my mind to wonder into darker places, I convinced myself I was the worse writer in the world.

It was really hard for me to keep writing but, I did it for me not for anybody else. This is the one thing in my life that's gives me joy. I wondered if all the sleepless nights and research was worth it anymore. I often had headaches from spending too much time on my computer. I put lots into my first book, though I knew it wasn't really the best I still put my entire heart into it. I also quickly wrote an unreleased sequel but, I wasn't feeling it anymore. I hid my depression as well as I could for an entire year, my dream was kind of crushed in a matter of months. I didn't put everything into this book as I normally would but, I hope it is still enjoyable. Writing nowadays is hard for me every time I try. I don't think I am nor do I claim to be a great writer but, I hope someone finds some enjoyment in these little creepy stories.

CONTENTS:

DEFIANT HAZEN

CHAPTER 1:

DO NOT GO GENTLE

In the distant future, the world is similar to the way it is now. Technology has reached new heights and achievements. It was more than normal that someone would depend on their automated driver as well, humans had almost forgotten how to drive on their own. Hazen Reams practically jumped into her backseat, backpack in hand. She pushed her hair out of her face as she yelled her drive command "Centrycar eight four two, fastest route to the hospital on fourth!" Before she could buckle up the car started and turned onto the street. She buckled herself in. She noticed her shirt was on backwards. "Seriously" she mumbled. She had overslept once again, she hoped she wouldn't get fired over being twenty minutes late again.

Hazen knew she had a ten-minute ride if the traffic was good. She pulled out her laptop and scanned her hand. She had to try to remember to scan in her memories as much as possible. Hazen knew she was forgetful, so she tried to scan in her memories every time she sat in the car. "Ms. Reams a small traffic jam is a mile ahead of us, what would you like me to do?" She watched the steering wheel move back in forth for a while. "The fastest route I don't care how you get me there!" The car swerved over into the next lane. Hazen grabbed her phone, she smiled at the message from her little brother Ian. She sent him back a quick good morning message. She smiled back at the picture he had sent her. "Centrycar put in an order at that bakery Ian always talks about... order a dozen vanilla truffles." Hazen tried to fix her hair with her fingers "I might get fired for how gross my hair looks."

"Two minutes until arrival Ms. Reams." She smiled upon seeing the hospital. The loud sounds of tires screeching made her stop in thought. She felt as if she was in the air then she felt the impact. Pain overtook her body, she couldn't see. It felt like she hit her head but, she wasn't sure it happened so fast. She felt the glass break against her skin. More honking followed then the broken voice box of Centrycar mumbled out something but, she never heard it.

One week later, the Reams family received a light knock on their door. Mr. Reams reluctantly opened the door himself. A cheery girl smiled brightly "Mr. Reams I presume?" He seemed surprised at the fact that she didn't use the automatic hologram system. "What can I do for you today?" She held out her hand "I'm Courtney, I work for CentryBot." Ian looked up from the couch because of the mention of CentryBot. "Sorry I didn't order anything and I don't want to buy another machine." Courtney turned her tablet around "I don't think you understand sir...we only specialize in replacement robots." She pointed to the name at the top of the file "Hazen Reams used our replacement after death program." Ian jumped up from the couch, the mere mention of her name almost caused him to go into a rage. Mr. Reams leaned against the doorframe after his legs became weak "what...what is that?" Courtney frowned "may I come in and explain our services?" "Please, come in...Ian go get your mother." Ian shook his head "dad... she said replacement." "Ian go, I won't ask again!"

The Reams sat around the kitchen table awaiting to find out what Courtney had to say. She pushed a button on her tablet to create a hologram video. "Hazen Reams was a part of our replacement program, a few years ago she signed up for our program." "Now our program is very unique, as often as possible we ask our clients to send in their memories as often as they can...Hazen did her last memory scan a few minutes before her death." Ian stood up "I don't need to know about that part, I know my sister died!" Courtney flinched "I apologize." "I hate all of this, my sister died because some guy's automatic driver busted so he attempted to drive himself...stupid people can't even remember how to drive!" "Sit down Ian" his mother yelled! Ian gulped "sorry, I'm still just angry." She smiled "I know baby but, let her finish."

Courtney cleared her throat "we provide a complete replica of Hazen down to the amount of hairs on her head." "Complete with all of her memory's, it'll be just like Hazen is back with you." Mrs. Reams covered her mouth "why would Hazen do this?" She scrolled over to the written apology Hazen had written. She started reading the small paragraph "if this is being read sadly, I must have died before my time, I love you all very much and I couldn't leave Ian all alone." She took a small pause "I don't want you all to miss me, just pretend the CentryBot is me...so you'll be happy."

Courtney closed the file "Hazen added the quote; I don't know what has caused me to make this decision." She held the tablet firmly to her chest "shall I bring in Hazen?" Ian had to bite his tongue so he wouldn't cuss at the mention of that thing being his sister. Mrs. Reams sighed "it was Hazen's wish, yeah… we'll try it out." Ian angrily sat down as Courtney went outside to retrieve the Hazen replacement. Ian's dad touched his shoulder lightly "I know this is hard and you're completely against it but, it doesn't sound that bad." "Dad a robotic version of my sister is about to come through the door, it's completely misguided."

It wasn't long before the door was opening. Courtney opened the door "Hazen this is your family…the Reams." Ian's mouth dropped open as the skinny dark-haired girl walked in. Hazen looked around the house as she walked towards the Reams. Mrs. Reams knees gave out "she looks just like our baby." Hazen smiled cheerfully and waved "because it is me... mom." Ian couldn't help his eyes from watering. He knew CentryBot's were supposed to look real but, this was incredible. Hazen knelt down by Mrs. Reams "mom let me help you up." Hazen gently put a hand on her back and held out her hand. She grabbed ahold of Hazen's hand; she was shocked by how lifelike her skin felt. She looked every bit as normal as a normal human, the only sign of technology was the small bright light on the side of her forehead. Her dark hair was the exact length as Hazen's even her clothes looked like something Hazen would have worn. Hazen's smile grew "Ian" she wrapped her arms around him "my baby brother, I love you so much!"

He nervously tightened his arm around her "she even has body heat." Courtney shook her head "our bots our completely lifelike most people can't tell the deference between a humans touch and the touch of a CentryBot. Ian slowly pulled away, he held in his tears "I can't...Hazen just died, I can't." He ran away to his room. Hazen seemed confused "what does Ian mean I didn't die, I'm right here." Mr. Reams put his arm around her "he's had a rough day, can you eat?" She shook her head "duh dad how else can I survive?" He almost lost his composer and cried but, he was able to hold himself together quite well.

Courtney left Hazen with the family and headed to the next drop off. Ian stayed in his room for the remainder of the day, he had trouble sleeping because he thought he saw Hazen's face light glowing from behind his curtains. He wasn't going to check his window in the middle of the night so he tried his best to ignore it. He came out of his room for breakfast the next day. Laughter was coming from the kitchen. He knew why but, he was hungry so he ignored how he felt. Hazen was laughing as his dad finished flipping a pancake. His mom was putting Hazen's graduation necklace back on her neck. Hazen smiled "oh I thought I lost it" she giggled. Ian sat down and stabbed a pancake with his fork "no we took it off of you when you died." "Ian stop it" his mother demanded "don't talk like that to your sister!" He almost choked on his pancake "excuse me...did you forget that she's a robot?" She rolled her eyes as she pushed some hair out of Hazen's face "were just happy she's safe with us." Hazen stuffed her mouth with pancakes "Ian, you aren't being a very nice brother lately...did I do something

11

wrong?" He continued eating to avoid the question.

Ian finished his breakfast "I'll walk to school today." He did this often and the junior high was just a few blocks over. His mom acted like she didn't notice as she kissed Hazen's head and continued pampering her. "My sweet girl, I love that you're home" she said. Hazen grabbed her moms' hand "mom are you okay...you seem to be sad?" "No...no I'm just so happy I have a daughter." Hazen's smile faded a little when she heard Ian leave. She got up calmly "I have to make sure Ian stays safe." "Honey, he'll be fine he walks that way all the time" her dad stated. She ignored his words "my main job is to protect Ian" her voice was calm but serious. She opened the door and located Ian. She stayed far behind him as he walked. Ian was happy to be out of the house, far away from the robot pretending to be his beloved sister. He cupped his mouth as he began to cry. He had been holding it in all night. He couldn't properly grieve with a walking imposter sharing his bathroom.

He knew his parents were in denial and were just playing family with the robot. Losing their first born had hit them hard, he knew the robot looked and acted enough like Hazen for them to ignore the fact that she wasn't real. He tried to keep his cries quiet so he didn't show the whole block that he was in pain. His heart felt as if it briefly stopped as he approached Andy Scouts house. He usually would have left by now. It appeared he was having some kind of car trouble. Ian tried to keep his head pointed at the ground, hoping to be ignored. Andy wasn't a terrible guy he just took his jokes and playing tactics a little too far most of the time.

He was someone Ian wanted to avoid at all costs. Andy was starting college soon so he really shouldn't have been picking on an eighth grader but, Andy was also a little dumb.

He noticed Ian, he tripped over his own shoe as he ran over to him. "Hey I saw the CentryBot people were at your house yesterday...what was that about?" He knew Andy was just curious but, honestly it wasn't any of his business. Ian wiped his eyes "yeah they were but, they left quickly so don't worry about it okay?" Andy shook his head "yeah alright" he gently pushed Ian "so why you crying?" Ian rubbed his arm "allergies" he tried to step around Andy "I need to get to school." Andy stepped in front of Ian and put his hands on his shoulder's "something seems to be up with you?" Ian pushed his hands off of him "leave me alone please." Ian said it quiet but, Hazen was still able to hear it.

It seemed like Hazen came out of nowhere, Ian hadn't even realized she was anywhere near him. She angerly walked towards him Andy "did you just hurt my brother!" Andy's eyes widened "oh crap...that's what happened your dead sister was replaced with one of those CentryBots!" Hazen ignored Andy "Ian are you harmed?" He shook his head "no, I'm fine...were you following me?" "Yes" she stepped in front of Ian. "I saw you put your hands on my brother...I have to protect Ian" her voice slowed "you have to be dealt with." She grabbed Andy's wrist and twisted it back. Andy's scream knocked Ian out of his confused trance. "Hazen stop it" he yelled! The anger on her face surprised him. Andy tried to pull away from her but, she was too strong. "Get your sister off of me" he begged. Ian tried to loosen her grip. "Ian, he has to be punished for hurting you." "No, he doesn't he didn't do anything, you can't go around breaking people's arms!" She failed to understand his reasoning "but, I have to protect you Ian." She spoke calmly as she continued twisting back his wrist. Ian gaged upon hearing Andy's wrist make a loud popping noise.

"Hazen, he didn't hurt me why should he be punished?" She crinkled her nose "I don't know ...but, I know I...have to protect you." Ian grabbed her face and looked at her eyes "my sister Hazen would never hurt anybody like this" he took a deep breath "I thought you were my sister." She stopped twisting his arm. He could see that she was searching her thoughts and memories. "You are right... Ian, I would never do this." She dropped Andy "I am sorry Andy...I checked my memories and found that you often do partake in this kind of behavior." Ian was able to breathe again, he held onto his chest "Andy how bad is it?" Andy didn't answer he was so traumatized by what had just transpired. Ian glanced down at his wrist; it was pointing the wrong way. The sight of it made his stomach turn.

He knelt down "Andy...hey can you hear me?" Hazen calmly stood up straight "I think he might just be in shock." Ian shouted "duh Hazen you almost tore off his hand, what the hell was that?" Hazen shook her head "I told you I have to protect you always." Ian felt a chill go down his spine when she spoke. He grabbed his phone and called 911. "It's going to be okay...Andy." Ian stared up at her, she was just staring down at him. He felt uneasy, this robot looked exactly like his sister but, what was inside wasn't right. "Go back home, he's afraid...

he shouldn't have to look at you" Ian yelled! He cradled Andy as he awaited the ambulance. Andy stared at Hazen as she walked away. The next call Ian made was to his mother, he hoped this incident would be enough to get them to send her back.

CHAPTER 2:

SISTER STALKER

Ian stayed with Andy until the ambulance came. He told the police what had happened. They told him to go to school like normal. They would get in contact with his parents to see what would have to be done about Hazen. He hoped they wouldn't be given a choice and Hazen would be taken away from them. He hated that that thing was tarnishing his sister's name. He couldn't stay focused on his schoolwork the entire day. When his lunch period came, he was relived. He ran out into the hall, he stopped. He fell against the wall, groups of kids walked past him. He shook his head "I'm just seeing things." He swore he had seen Hazen standing on the other side of the wall. He rubbed his eyes "no I just need to stop thinking about her." He motioned for his friend Zen to come to him. The short boy made his way over to Ian. "You okay, you look ill?" "Yeah don't worry about me, Zen did you by any chance do your algebra homework?" Zen shook his head "of course I did." Ian had forgotten all about it once the robot had shown up. "Good I need to copy it."

They found a place to sit at lunch, their normal table at the far end of the cafeteria. He vented his story to Zen while he was copying down algebra problems. Zen seemed terrified "well you know we always joke about *Skynet* but..." Ian felt a chill go up his spine "don't joke like that today." Zen started gulping down the plain potatoes and mixed vegetables on his tray. Ian turned his head sharply towards the window. "Ian you seem like you're still freaked out" he rubbed his head "it's that robot isn't it?" Zen sighed "come on Ian I'm sure there is some type of failsafe thing on CentryBot's" he whispered "after *Terminator* I think everyone has distrusted AI's and technology." "I swear I saw Hazen standing behind me" he shook as if he was uncomfortable. Zen grabbed his phone "I highly doubt that, the police and CentryBot are looking for her right now." "Ian look" he showed him a webpage on his phone "look on the CentryBot website it says if any bot becomes unstable break their neck... they have a weak lining on them made specifically for this, it should popoff easily." Ian looked at the diagram "I'm sure the company will deal with her I'm not worried about having to shut down the robot."

Zen shrugged "I don't know might be good to know this information" he put his phone away. Ian's hands started shaking. Zen panicked "what...what is it?" Ian pushed his phone towards Zen "Hazen's calling me." Ian's face filled with panic "what do I do?" Zen grabbed the phone and put it on speaker "hello." The line was silent for a few seconds then Hazen spoke. "Ian, I need you to come home with me, you aren't safe here." Ian swallowed hard "yes I am, Hazen you need to go home" he tried to hide his shaky voice "they need you to be home." "No Ian, mom and dad are safe at home however, you aren't." Ian froze so Zen decided to speak up for him "Hazen its Zen do you remember me?" She answered quickly "yes, Ian's best friend." Zen looked over at Ian who was noticeable angry and scared at the same time. "Ian is safe with me; he will be home later." "No, he will leave now...I am coming to get you Ian." Zen hung up "that was terrifying" he stood up and put his backpack on "come on Ian you have to run!"

Ian thought for a second "where should I go?" Zen grabbed his arm and took off running. He ignored the screaming teachers. "Ian, I think you should try to get home before Hazen, if we go through the gym, we can be closer to your house." Zen pulled hard against Ian's hand "come on if she's as strong as you say she's probably fast as well." Ian tried not to show how afraid he was but, he knew Zen could sense it. The sounds of boots banging against the tile floor behind them sent a sense of panic through their hearts. Ian flashed back to the morning, he remembered Hazen had on her favorite combat boots. A pit began to grow in his stomach as he and Zen ran as fast as they could into the gym. Zen stopped to lock the doors. He grabbed ahold of Ian's hand again and pulled him towards the opposite side of the gym "okay Ian go!" "Zen why aren't you coming with me?"

Zen opened his mouth to speak but, stopped once he heard the loud bang at the door. Both boys looked at the door as Hazen slammed her palm against it. Zen pushed Ian towards the door "go already!" With one final slam the gym door bent. Hazen pushed it open as if it was no trouble. Ian pushed open the gym door "come on Zen seriously she might kill you!" Hazen calmly spoke "Ian why are you running away from me

I'm your sister?" Ian felt his hands start to shake "Zen please." Zen stood back "I have to distract her...hurry up!" Ian closed his eyes and ran through the door and started running across the parking lot. He stopped running when he heard the first of Zen's screams.

Zen tried to cover his mouth as she yanked his arm back. "Did you hurt my brother...why were you taking him away from me?" Zen could feel his eyes watering "I was protecting him." Hazen pulled back on his arm and stretched it "protect him from what?" Ian slung the door open "from you Hazen drop him now!" He didn't wait for her to comply instead he threw his backpack as hard as he could at her. The backpack hit her in the face hard. She dropped Zen. Zen grabbed his arm. "Hazen I'm going home you better come with me to protect me!" Ian pushed the door open and ran out, he kept his pace slow until he heard the door slam back open. He ran as fast as he could, he didn't know how fast she was but, he hoped he was faster. He thought it was strange that his parents hadn't even thought about texting him. He shook the thought and ran. He ran across the road without looking for cars.

"Ian stop it you're going to get hurt!" He heard her scream from behind him. He ignored it as he turned down his street. He could see his dad's car in the driveway. He felt a little bit of fear lift off of his heart. Ian pulled his keycard out of his pocket. He ran across the yard; he went to scan his keycard on the door. He filled with panic as the door rejected his key. His eyes widened "what's going on!" His pulse was up so high he could feel his brain pumping blood around his head. He tried it again but, once again it denied him. He felt a hand softly touch his back "Ian you need me to get into the house." His muscles tightened and he became stiff. Hazen put her finger over the sensor "only I can open it." The door slowly opened, she gently pushed him in.

Ian felt the pit in his stomach grow, the lump in his throat kept him from talking. Hazen closed the door behind him. "Don't worry Ian I'm only doing this for your safety." Ian swallowed hard "where's mom?" Hazen blinked "sounds like she's still in the kitchen, I told her to make you something for lunch...I was sure you'd be hungry." Ian agreed "I am hungry" he said calmly. "And dad?" Hazen listened for a second "I can hear him walking around upstairs." She sat down in the living room "go eat your lunch and maybe we can find a movie or something." He quickly walked to the kitchen. His mother seemed relieved to see him. Ian ran to his mom and whispered in her ear "what's going on?" "We were able to call CentryBot to tell them about the incident with Andy...she heard us and rewired the house somehow; we can't leave without her." Ian could barely make out his mom's teary whisper. She handed him a sandwich "eat this before she gets upset."

Ian grabbed the sandwich. He talked in between bites "so what did CentryBot say?" She looked towards the door "they said they would send someone to retrieve her because she's obviously defective." Ian shrugged "I'd say she was defiant...mom what if they can't get in because of what Hazen did?" Her eyes grew "we'll deal with that later, just pretend like you don't know anything." He finished the sandwich "just stay away from her, if she thinks you're bad for me she'll hurt you." Ian tried to stop his hands from shaking as he sat next to Hazen. Hazen smiled "what do you want to watch" she handed him the remote. Ian smirked "doesn't matter." He forced out a smile "you used to like that one old show...what was it called?" Hazen lit up "oh *Friends* you mean!" She smiled and grabbed the remote from him "yeah I want to watch that!" The cheer in her voice almost matched that of his sister's. He frowned as he looked at her. She looked like his sister, even acted like her but, her human element was gone...Hazen was gone.

She smiled as she finally found the show in the old TV archives. The small light on her head slowly blinked. It made him physically sick to see the robot wearing his sisters face. An hour had passed since Ian had returned home; his parents were now also in the living area pretending to enjoy watching the show. Everyone turned towards the door as they heard a knock. Mr. Reams leapt up. Hazen smiled "dad, I got it...sit down." He did as he was told. Hazen opened the door and smiled "why Miss Courtney what are you doing here?" She smiled "Hazen may I come in for a second, I need to talk to you?" Hazen seemed reluctant but, she allowed her to come in. Courtney shook her head "Hazen we've had two violent incidents reported to us about you in the last five hours." Hazen's smile faded "I was protecting my brother." She sighed "Hazen I need you to come with me so we can see if something went wrong in your programming, you should be back by tomorrow." She shook her head "no miss I won't leave Ian to be defenseless...I have to protect him."

Courtney frowned "no Hazen you need to come with me, your family will be safe." Hazen glanced back at her family "no...I know the protocol for out of control bots...I'll be destroyed!" She seemed confused "Hazen where are you getting this information?" "Miss, I remember my time in the lab before I was born as Hazen." Courtney gulped "that's rather odd" she started pushing some buttons on her tablet. Hazen touched her necklace "this is my family; I have to make sure they aren't harmed." She dropped her arms "you taking me will cause them harm."

She knocked the tablet from her hands and grabbed ahold of Courtney's neck. Ian yelled "Hazen don't!" Hazen pushed a choking Courtney up against the door as she lifted her up "I have to stay and protect Ian." Mr. Reams ran over and tried pulling Hazen's hand away from her neck. It made little impact as she closed her hand tighter around her neck.

Courtney kicked at Hazen as she tried her hardest to pull her hands from her throat. "Hazen if you really are my sister let her go" he touched her shoulder "my sister would never kill anything!" Hazen tightened her grip as she began to go blue in the face "incorrect I would do anything to protect my brother."

CHAPTER 3:

STOP PRETENDING TO BE MY SISTER

Hazen spent the night cleaning up the murder she carried out on the CentryBot employee. Ian didn't sleep at all. She took away all the phones in the house. She also disconnected all of the house's other technological equipment. Hazen wouldn't tell them what happened to Courtney's body. Ian and his parents sat around the kitchen table, staring at each other. Hazen entered the room, they all jumped. Mrs. Reams rubbed her eyes "Hazen don't you think we should all get dressed and go to Andy's house...we promised his parents we'd all be over to apologize." Hazen simply frowned instead of giving an answer. Ian looked at his parents his mother was petrified, he was sure he could hear her heartbeat. His dad didn't look much better, the sweat was rolling off of his forehead in sheets.

Ian had seen enough old sci-fi movies to figure out that it was only a matter of time before Hazen grew more paranoid which meant more dangerous. He stood up, he tried to keep his hands as still as possible while he poured himself some juice. He turned his face away from his parents so they couldn't see his expressions. "Hey Hazen, can I ask a favor of you?" Her eyes opened up wider "Ian as long as it's not dangerous." Her sweet voice made him feel uneasy "I think I want to rearrange my room; I can't lift much weight." She smiled "I'm strong enough to help!" Mrs. Reams almost stood up "Ian." "Mom can you and dad make us something for breakfast" he finished his juice "we'll be back down in a few minutes."

She sighed "Ian...don't, just be..." Hazen shrugged "mom it really isn't any trouble, dad I think I want pancakes again" she smiled. Mr. Reams stood up from the table "anything for my sweet girl." Ian agreed knowing his dad sounded genuine. Ian took off upstairs "hurry Hazen." She seemed to be full of excitement. Ian ran into his room "okay so I have a few ideas." Hazen smiled kindly "whatever you want Ian." He pretended to think "maybe move the dresser by the closet...then we'll move the bed closer to the window" he forced out an overly happy grin "what do you think?"

She immediately grabbed ahold of the bed frame and pushed it against the wall and pulled it towards the window. Ian could feel his hands begin to sweat; his heart began to beat faster. Hazen finished messing with the bed and moved onto the dresser. Ian took a step closer to her, he stepped right behind her. He gasped "Hazen wait...your necklace!" She dropped the dresser creating a loud thud "what is it?" Ian squinted his eyes "its twisted in your hair, here allow me." He motioned for her to turn around "I know how important it is for you, remember we all went and picked it out at graduation?" She turned her back to him and lifted up her hair "yeah I remember you got food poising that day from that sticky bun thing" she giggled.

Ian grabbed ahold of the necklace; her giggle made him frown. "Hazen do you recall last Easter when we threw eggs at mom and she dropped potato salad on both are heads?" Hazen seemed puzzled "Ian…I don't remember that" she searched her memory banks "why can't I remember that event?" Ian pulled the necklace tighter in his hands "we'll that's because it didn't happen." Ian pulled the necklace to him. He felt the thick gold chain tighten in his fingers. Hazen gasped "Ian what are you doing?" She tried gently pulling at his fingers. He pulled up hard on the necklace and backed up a few steps. Hazen fell up against him. "Ian please…why would you hurt your sister?" Ian filled with more hatred; he could visibly see her neck starting to fray. She obviously didn't need air to breath but, she had to of known what he was trying to do.

Ian tightened the necklace as tight as possible; his fingers were sore and his hands couldn't stop shaking. A small part of him felt horrible for killing a clone of his sister. She begged "Ian please, why would you do...this?" Her words started being harder to understand as he used the necklace to cut away at her realistic skin base. He could feel wires starting to poke his fingers. "Ian...love...you" she tried to say. Ian yelled "how dare you...stop pretending to be my sister!" He used the last bit of strength he had to pull hard against her neck. Hazen's hands dropped as her head loosened and fell forward. Ian finished pulling the necklace through the wires on her neck. The light on Hazen's head flickered out. Ian held the necklace in his hands. He looked down at the still body of the CentryBot. "I did it" he whispered. He kicked her head to make sure she really was beheaded. He could feel his heartbeat return to normal. "She's gone, I did it!"

Later that day Ian convinced his dad to drive him to the cemetery while the police and CentryBot were cleaning out the house trying to find Courtney's remains. Ian made his dad wait in the car. He slowly walked over to the fresh grave. He knelt down by the flowers on top of the dirt covering her casket. "Hey sis" he mumbled. Ian pulled out Hazen's graduation necklace "we tried to do things like you wanted, we really did." He put his hand against the dirt "the hardest part of all of this was...me not doing what you wished of us." He started to choke up as his tears started pooling against his eyelids. "I miss you so much, that thing could never replace you" he felt peaceful talking to her grave as if she was still alive sitting next to him.

"Mom and dad miss you to, I think I miss you the most" he swallowed "you didn't get to see me fail at high school." He laid the necklace on the dirt "I'm sorry we took this from you Hazen." He tried his best to hold back his tears "everything's fine now...with the CentryBot I mean, I understand you just wanted to take care of me." He stood up "I love you, goodbye" he turned back to the car trying to show his dad how strong he had remained.

SPELLBOUND

CHAPTER:1

HOME TOGETHER

"Please officer..." The tired cop looked at me once again with complete disgust "Mr. Blanchard for the final time we have definitive proof that you killed your wife today, January 3, 1987." I shook my head, I put my cuffed hands on the desk "like I said the person I killed wasn't my wife!" I knew he was tired of hearing me spit out the same story but, I had to try and get my point across. He was already mad at the amount of tissues I had used in the last hour. "Alright once more Mr. Blanchard" he threw the case file at me "you killed Ginger Blanchard; we can prove that, what we need from you is the reason why?" I shook my head "I told you why?" "Yes, we know that's why I'm still sitting here wasting my night with you" he popped his jaw. I was getting fed up, he wasn't getting it "Tate disappeared after I killed her!" I couldn't stop myself from yelling. "So, you really want to stick with the crazy claim" he rubbed his forehead? "I am not crazy" I shouted. I took a deep breath "look this whole thing took place over four days...let me explain myself." I knew he wasn't feeling like listening to me any longer, I could see it in his eyes. "I'm already admitting my guilt...I just want to tell you why...can you listen...please." He rolled his eyes a little "proceed."

43

It started on December 31st. I had just gotten off late again, I had a crappy salesmen job but, it payed the rent. It was cold outside so I stayed in my car for a little while. As I tried to warm up, I noticed lots of lights were on in the house but, I'm thirty-three I never forgot to turn off the lights. My first guess was the landlord, she appeared to be attracted to me. She always stopped by for no reason except to talk. I wasn't immediately concerned. I got out of the car like I normally would. I pulled out my key but, the door was already opened. By this point I'm thinking landlord. Then once I walk in, I smell this horrible smell like burnt popcorn. I rush to the kitchen because somethings obviously burning. In my kitchen I find a gorgeous blonde woman, which most people would agree is a good thing but, I never saw this woman before in my life and she was cooking in my kitchen. Then she smiled at me and yells out "Marcel you're finally here!" I looked at her like she's crazy but, she's looking at me like she's ready to jump into my arms.

So, I nervously ask her "lady who are you and how'd you get into my house?" She looked at me offended. "Marcel isn't it common for the wife to have her own key?" I almost lost my balance "wife... whose wife?" She stood there for a second with her mouth open "umm your wife dummy...Ginger Blanchard!" By this point I am thinking about a practical joke by one of my family members but, then I see it. A picture of my entire family at what looks like my wedding only I've never been married, I honestly don't think I've ever even seen the wedding location. I felt dizzy, my heart began to pound. Ginger frowned "need pain pills dear?" I shook my head "yeah any pills will do" I ended up leaning against the counter. Ginger brought me more of my usual pain pills as if she knew the ones I always took.

She watched me take them before kissing the top of my head "are you ready for dinner?" I rubbed my eyes "umm...I still need to figure out how this happened." Before Ginger could answer me, someone came in through the front door. He laid himself out on my couch. I clearly could see him from where I was leaning. "Who are you?" He rolled his eyes and kicked off his high tops "funny dad, you are hilarious." I grabbed at my chest as the shock hit me "dad me...oh no..." I turned back at Ginger "so he comes with you?" She ignored me and started plating food. The boy cut on the TV "double feature tonight dad, *He knows you're alone* and *The Funhouse.*" He seemed super excited. I tried to process what I just heard "you like horror movies I guess?" Ginger laughed "Tate has seen every horror movie at least twice." I gulped "Tate...your name is Tate?" He turned up the volume on the TV "my friend got a *Sleepaway Camp* tape; I'll probably go get it later."

I sat down on the barstool by the counter "Ginger and Tate...wife and son." My head started spinning, I knew I never seen these people before. It's not possible I repeated to myself. My mind was spinning, I felt sick to my stomach. I looked around there was more pictures on the wall of me, Ginger and Tate. The house did have a feminine touch, it looked much different than it did this morning when I left. That's it I thought, I took to many pain pills with my sleeping pills last night and I'm having a fever dream or something. That makes more sense. Ginger put a plate of what looked like pot-roast in front of me. I sighed realizing that was where the burnt smell was coming from. I shrugged, probably just a weird dream. I poked at the tough meat. Ginger smiled "eat up honey!" Her perkiness tricked me into trying the food. It was horrible, honestly the worst thing I ever ate. It was more than just burnt; the flavor was otherworldly.

Ginger gave Tate a plate of food, he immediately started eating it as if the flavor didn't seem to bother him at all. I didn't want to hurt her feelings but, it was so repulsive I couldn't possibly stomach it. I wiped my mouth "I feel kind of sick I'm going to go lay down. Ginger frowned "I can bring you some food later." I shook my head "no I think I'm just going to get to sleep." Hopefully this strange dream would end once I laid down. I had strange dreams a few times from my pills but, never anything this weird.

A few hours later Ginger came in with some water "feeling better?" I could feel my eyes open as if I actually fell asleep. I looked around the room in a bit of a panic, the whole room was pink and covered in white flowers. I defiantly didn't know where any of this stuff had come from. Was it possible to forget big chunks of your own life? Ginger sat next to me Marcel are you okay...did you mix your pills again?" I shook my head; I put on a pair of my comfortable shoes and grabbed a coat from the closet. "I have to go get something real fast." She seemed surprised "but, Marcel its midnight?" I ignored her and grabbed my keys. Tate was still watching TV. He chugged a can of soda as I walked by. I noticed the starting credits of *Prom Night* as I closed the door. I ran to my car; I could already feel my tears running down my face. I had always cried a lot so I had learned when it was coming. I started my car "what the hell is going on here!" I started driving as I argued with myself "how can I have a family that I don't remember?" My breathing was elevated "I feel like I just woke up, how is that possible if this is all a dream?"

I managed to stop crying once I pulled up to the police station. I jumped out of my car and ran into the police station. The receptionist seemed shocked by how fast I ran in. "Sir can I help you with something?" I pulled out my I.D "there is a woman and boy in my house, I have no idea who they are!" She grabbed my I.D "alright hold on Mr. Blanchard." She left me and came back within a few minutes with another officer. He had a folder with him. I rubbed my eyes "are you going to head over to my house?" The officer looked at me "sir who is the woman and boy in your house?" I shrugged "I have no idea like I said I never saw them before." "Ginger and Tate are the names they gave me" I noticed he was reading something in the file. "Mr. Blanchard your wife Ginger called less than five minutes ago because she was worried you took too many sleeping pills...she asked us to keep a lookout for your car."

My mouth dropped open "she isn't my wife!" "Oh really" the officer said. He handed me the folder "because last month Marcel Blanchard and Ginger Blanchard came in to get a restraining order to protect your son Tate Blanchard from a bully in his class." I gulped as I read the document. As far as the document said Ginger was legally my wife and Tate was my son. I dropped the file on the desk "but, I don't remember this...or my so-called wife." The officer didn't seem pleased. "So, you did ingest a large amount of sleeping pills, didn't you?" I didn't want to answer but, I did anyways "yeah I took sleeping pills but, I don't think that can make me forget two whole people!" The officer shook his head "you would be surprised sir; by how much pills influence our outlook." He grabbed me by my arm and turned me around "sir you are not driving, you will stay here until your wife comes to pick you up." I bit my lip "she isn't my wife!" He ignored me as he handcuffed me to one of the desks "sir you obviously need to go see a doctor."

Twenty minutes later Ginger came strolling through the police station. She knelt down by me "oh my poor honey" she rubbed my hands "officer please let my husband out." She seemed like she was really worried about me. How could I forget someone as pretty as her

I thought? She seemed so nice but, the only explanation was she was crazy or I was. I didn't think I could be the crazy one but, looking at all the evidence I slightly started to doubt my own story. An officer came by and uncuffed me. Ginger was allowed to take me home, she said she'd come get her car in the morning. As she drove me back home my mind began to put more of the pieces together. I knew as of yesterday I was still sane. People can't completely forget everything within a few hours...it wasn't possible.

I glanced over at her as she drove "Ginger...where did you get a car, there was no car in the driveway when I got home?" She smiled a big toothy smile "honey Tate had it he went to the movies remember?" I thought back "no because whenever Tate came back there still wasn't any car in the driveway when I left." I knew it, I screamed in my thoughts. I had found it, a flaw; I wasn't losing my mind something strange was going on. "Tate is a very hard sleeper so he won't hear us coming in" she said as she changed the radio to some type of classical music. "Speaking of Tate, if we have a son...I'm guessing about sixteen, why would we only have a one-bedroom house?" She shrugged "Tate doesn't mind sleeping on the sofa...that way he can watch his movies late into the night." I wasn't buying it, I started to crack away at this fake façade.

Ginger stayed silent the rest of the way home, she wouldn't answer any of my questions and she refused to look my way. Once we arrived home, she acted super attentive towards me. More than she did previously. She opened the door for me, we walked past Tate who was passed out across the couch holding a pillow to his head. Ginger grabbed me a box of crackers from the kitchen "honey I think you should eat a snack and try to go to bed." I took the crackers and ate them, I was starving. I went back into the room mainly so I could think. I knew Ginger and Tate didn't belong in my house, that was clear. I didn't know what to do, I stuffed the remaining crackers into my mouth. The police couldn't do anything their influence had stretched to the police department. I couldn't get rid of them.

I looked over at the phone on the nightstand, maybe a few calls could clear some of this up I thought. I called my brother first. "Marcel...Marcel do you have any idea what time it is?" I glanced at the clock "almost 1:30am." He sounded mad but, I didn't care, at the moment I had worse problems. "Hey, did you ever meet my wife?" He was silent. I heard a yawn before he yelled. "Marcel seriously I have work tomorrow and you're playing games with me!" I shouted "did you meet my wife?" "Yeah stupid I was your best man...I guess next you're going to ask me if I ever met my nephew!" He went on and on about how he was just at dinner last week. I stopped listening as my heart dropped into my stomach. I hung up on him. My hands started sweating as I nervously pushed the buttons. I decided to call my mother, if this was some type of prank, she'd let me know. I knew she wouldn't let me suffer.

"Hello" she answered sleepily. "Mom it's Marcel." She sat up "are you alright it's late?" My hands shook as I tried my hardest to hold the phone "mom I'm scared, somethings going on and I don't understand." "Marcel what's wrong are you alright?" I rubbed my forehead "mom am I married...really married to a woman named Ginger...or is this just a joke?" She was silent. I heard her cut on a lamp. I sat there nervously as I awaited her answer. "I don't understand the question, Marcel are you and Ginger having marital problems...do I need to come pick up my grandson?" I felt tears roll down my face "so it spread to my family as well." I dropped the phone and screamed. My head started pounding from all my constant stress. I grabbed the pain pills I kept by my bed; I could still hear my mother talking. I downed a few pain pills. I grabbed the sleeping pills. "Maybe when I wake up my life will be back to normal." I took double the amount I was supposed to take. My eyes closed soon.

I was in and out of sleep for a few days, Ginger fed me and gave me water. I remember that much. I also remember seeing my mom, she looked so sad. Tate came in the room once or twice. By the time I was completely able to wake up it was January 2, at 8:00pm. I walked out of my room and was discouraged as I saw Ginger in the kitchen and Tate on the couch. I groaned as I leaned against the counter "can you people just get out of my house" I yelled! Ginger acted as if she didn't hear me and instead put a bowl of what I assumed was soup in front of me. I knew it would taste like hot garbage but, I tried it anyway. I couldn't spit it out fast enough. Her food tasted vile like a flavor I'd never even tasted. I tossed the bowl on the floor. She seemed shocked "Marcel you are really starting to bother me with this constant attitude." I walked over to the couch "well leave then!" I pointed at Tate "move over!" He crossed his arms and moved aside for me. I sat next to him and immediately recognized *My Bloody Valentine.* "How are you even finding all these slasher movies?"

He shrugged "because I want to watch them?" I grabbed the remote and changed it to the news "well, no more horror movies...you and your mom better leave before things get worse around here!" Tate stood up "mom why's dad acting like this?" I could feel the anger in me as I yelled "stop calling me dad you know I am not related to whatever you are...so stop with all of this!" I never was an anger person but, this was getting ridiculous. Ginger continued cleaning the soup off of the floor "Tate he's just under stress..." I leaped up "yeah, Ginger because you showed up knowing that you aren't married to me!" "I think I should go over to a friend's house" Tate said before walking out the door. "Good, don't

come back...why don't you follow him...
the cause of my stress is you...whatever
kind of thing you are..." She interrupted
me "now I shouldn't be talked to like
this, I am your wife!" "No, you are not"
I yelled! I kicked the sofa "fine I want a
divorce, get the hell out of here!" She
looked like she wanted to cry "Marcel
what did I do to deserve this?"

I could feel my blood pressure rising.
"Leave...leave...leave!" I walked up to
her and grabbed her shoulders "get
away from me and never come back!"
She tried to touch my face "is it the
sleeping pills...they mess with your brain
so much." Her kind voice didn't distract
me at all. I knew that it was all an act.
I pushed her hand away "don't touch
me, get out!" She argued at me calmly
for hours as I tried to get her to leave.
I was so frustrated I had started crying.
She never had one tear, her eyes stayed

the same, they seemed loving. Around midnight Tate finally came back. It was now January 3rd. He came back in and cut on the TV, this time *The Slumber Party Massacre* was on. I stormed off to the bathroom. My body ached and I had a migraine, I took a few pain pills. I didn't bother counting, I never did.

I soaked in the bath for about twenty minutes. I never was this mad in my entire life. My life hadn't been anything special but, I wanted it back. I wiped my eyes as tears started forming again. The pain pills weren't kicking in at all. I felt just as bad as I did before. I got up an searched my medicine cabinet for something stronger. I found a pill bottle with the name Ginger Blanchard on it. It was for a strong pain pill, I never heard of it but, it was well over a thousand milligrams. I took two, I hated pain. I had never been able to take pain. I dried off and grabbed a pair of pajama pants. I had never seen them before, much like everything in my house.

I walked into the living room; Ginger was fixing up the pantry. I rolled my eyes at the very sight of her. My vision blurred for a second. I was already feeling a lot better. I glanced at the TV; it was so loud I couldn't help it. One of the girls was getting drilled, literally. The girls screaming stopped as she died. I felt a sense of relief cover my entire body. If they won't leave, I can make them. I ran into the kitchen and searched all the drawers for something large, I didn't have a power drill but, I had a meat cleaver. They aren't real people, this isn't wrong they aren't real, I tried to tell myself.

I gripped the meat clever in my hand. The screams from the TV kept me going. My vision blurred again for only a second. I glanced at both of them. If I take out Ginger then Tate will most likely leave as well. The room was dark but, I could see clearly. I had to do it before I chickened out. I walked up behind her and grabbed a handful of her hair. She reacted to the pain, which was strange to me. I pulled her head back as hard as I could. I slammed her head against the counter. She screamed something about loving me. Tate was already on me trying to pull back my arm but, I was stronger. I brought my hand down as hard as I could. The meat clever clanked off of the other side of the counter. It went right through. Once I dropped her hair and backed away, she fell off of the counter and onto the ground.

I dropped the bloody clever. I gaged when I looked at my hand. "Why didn't she disappear?" I turned around to look at Tate, he was gone as if he disappeared into the air. I looked down at Ginger, she was bleeding so much. The blood was pouring out. "Why is she bleeding, she isn't real!" I turned to the sink and puked out the little that was in my stomach. I sat there waiting for her body to disappear for what seemed like hours but, then I heard police sirens.

I had finished my story, I didn't know what the police officer thought but, I knew he didn't seem to believe my explanation. "Look Mr. Blanchard, do you hear yourself?" He didn't let me answer before he got up and left the room. I filled with panic; they think Ginger is real...what if I go to prison for this? I could feel my chest tightening. Why couldn't they see it, she can't really be dead because she isn't real. Another police officer came in along with the one that had been interrogating me. He had his own folder as well. "My associate found some interesting things; I think you should hear." He went right into it "so when you got here, I looked at your body." "Sir you have abnormal bleeding and bruising all over your body, and with your account of what happened and the same story given to us by the witness..." "What witness" I yelled. He finished without answering me.

"That bruising should be impossible and your fast eye movements are giving you away, the lab will tell me for sure but, it seems you were plenty high when you committed this crime." "No, that's not it...I have a thing with pain" I tried to sound as sincere as I could. My body was aching. The police officer was tired of listening to me, I could tell. They both looked at me. "He closed up his file "look we have a confession from you and a witness, we're done here." The first cop got up and left. I felt another wave of tears coming. "Mr. Blanchard, I want you to know while you were in here talking up a storm, we found your son." My head slowly fell against the desk, I thought he had finally left. "I wanted him to disappear, why would he come back, he left!" The officer slammed his hands on the desk, making me pull my head off. "Tate might have died along with his mother if he hadn't run off to a friend's house." The officer was visibly upset "you're a monster...you would have killed your own son if he hadn't escaped!"

I shook my head in disagreement "no, look I know how this looks but, I don't have a son and I'm not married!" The officer stood up and grabbed my cuffed hands "this isn't going anywhere." He pulled me out of the interrogation room. He wasn't being gentle with me at all. As

I was being pulled, I caught a glance of my mother holding Tate in her arms. I pulled away from the officer and yelled out "get away from my mother, I don't know what you are!" I felt someone grab ahold of my shirt. I was slammed against the wall as they restrained me further. I saw the look on my mother's face, it was pure disgust. Was she feeling that for me, why would she I was the one who should be full of disgust? I tried to fix my life but, it didn't work. I was pushed into a cell. "I don't deserve to be in here" I shouted!

They left me alone in the cell, all alone. I smiled a little at the idea of being alone for a while. This is what I wanted all along. I sat down on the floor, I wondered if I'd be able to sleep without my sleeping pills ever again. What about my pain pills I thought, what if I have bad pain? My head was already pounding. Was it normal for me to be worried about pain pills instead of my freedom? I tried to relax against the wall, I was so tired. I couldn't wait to drift off into a deep sleep.

THE SNAKE MAN

CHAPTER 1:

SNAKE IN THE GRASS

I slammed the door open "Lewis seriously?" I knew he was obviously drunk again. He could barely keep his head up. His bangs were falling into his face as he tried to make eye contact with me. I rolled my eyes "Lewis..." He fell back asleep. I purposely stomped on the ground as I rattled the travel trailer. I kicked his foot "Lewis wake up!" He flinched back and held his head "Elyse why are you yelling at me?" His tone of voice made me angry "because once again you didn't do anything that I asked of you, on your days off I wish you would do something besides get drunk!"

He rolled his eyes and covered his mouth "seriously?" "Yeah, seriously" I flared my nostrils up at him. I pointed my finger in his face "come on Lewis we don't love each other we're just glorified roommates!" "I think we just need to separate from each other... before we end up hating each other." He sprang up, I never saw him move so fast "Elyse where is all of this coming from?" I backed up a little, there wasn't much space in the trailer for verbal arguments but, I knew I didn't have a choice. "When we first started dating things were different, when you moved in everything went to hell" I rubbed my temples "Lewis please...start looking for a place to live." "I don't want to be in a relationship with you anymore...you can stay..." Lewis got close to me "no."

"No, what do you mean no?" Lewis's eyes slanted; I never saw them do that before. "We don't break up until I am done" he pushed back his bangs to show off his green eyes. He didn't frighten me "Lewis I am done, don't push me...I push back!" He seemed surprised by my words. He got closer to me, I frowned "Lewis you don't clean, you barely work and to be very honest you aren't good at being a boyfriend" I poked his chest "either accept it or leave my property!" I tried to hold back my anger "this is the last straw and I can't take living like this anymore!" He turned away from me "then maybe you shouldn't live."

I pushed him back as hard as I could, his drunk self-stumbled back onto the couch. "Are you threating me, seriously!" I couldn't believe the audacity. I walked into my bedroom and grabbed my shotgun, I always kept it loaded. You do that when you live in the country. I pointed it at his chest "get out!" He didn't like that at all "I decide when this is over." I interrupted him "no actually you don't...leave now or I'll shoot you where you sit!" he stood slowly "you really don't want to do that Elyse." I opened the door for him and swerved out of his way "no I do, you just proved that you aren't worth anymore of my time." He didn't scare me but, I never trusted people so I jumped to extreme measures before they would.

He slowly walked past me; I noticed his jaw clench. I kept my finger on the trigger. Lewis jumped down onto the ground "Elyse this won't end like..." I slammed the door in his face and locked it. I thought about calling the police but, I changed my mind. I sat down on the couch and took a deep breath. I knew Lewis wasn't perfect by any means but, I didn't think he would threaten me like that. I put the gun on my lap. I wanted to wait for his car to start before I went back outside. The gentle breeze from the open windows calmed me. I was genuinely relieved that he was gone, I hadn't cared for him for a while. We never really had a loving relationship, it used to be a lot better though. I shook the memories. I wondered why his car hadn't started up yet.

Before I could get up from the couch, I felt something slide across my collarbone. I flinched for a second but, threw it off. I gasped at the sight of the snake that was now crawling on my floor. I hit the butt of my shotgun on the ground lightly and crushed its head. I rubbed my eyes "what are the odds of that happening today of all days?" I turned to the window to look out, still confused on how the snake climbed up the wall. I stuck my head out the window, I was immediately confused by what I saw. Several snakes were slithering through the grass, headed right for my trailer. I had never seen so many snakes in one place. I closed the window. "What is this?" While I was focused on the window, I felt an intense pain emulate from my ankle. I clenched my jaw as the pain shot through my leg. I looked down as another snake slithered under the couch.

I panicked a little and grabbed my gun, I didn't know what kind of snake had bitten me. I had been bitten before but, some venom was more toxic then others. I knew Lewis was still outside but, I needed to get to the hospital. With the luck I was having it was probably going to be lethal. I gripped onto my gun as I opened the door. I jumped back once the door opened. Several more snakes swarmed around my door as if to keep me trapped. Lewis was leaning against his car, smiling coldly. "Lewis aren't you concerned with the number of snakes?" He didn't answer instead he just walked towards me. "Lewis don't walk around the snakes!" He ignored me as he calmly walked around the snakes. They didn't slither away or try to bite him. He stood near the door, staring at me. I held on firmly to my shotgun "Lewis."

He leaned closer; I moved my head away as he leaned in the doorway. I blinked rapidly when I noticed his teeth. He hardly ever smiled but, he was smiling from ear to ear. I never noticed that he had fangs, they were tiny but, obviously they were there. I tried not to look at them. "Are you trying to figure out something?" His tone was so irritating to me. I could feel my leg throbbing. "Lewis move, I need to go to the hospital." He shrugged "snake bite?" I was stunned "how do you..." I looked him in his eyes "are you doing this?" He held onto the door to balance himself "well what do you think Elyse?" I dropped my guard as I looked at his small fangs poking out from under his lip. He grabbed my gun and pulled it out of my hands. He quickly tossed it behind him. It landed near his car. My nearest neighbor was almost two miles away, if he hurt me nobody would ever know.

I stumbled back as he jumped towards me. He grabbed ahold of my arm as I lost my balance. His grip was strong. I fell onto my back. He pushed up against me

"Elyse do you regret…" I slapped him as hard as I could "I don't regret anything; you aren't worth my time." I knew that was stupid to say but, everything about him was angering me. He wrapped his hand around my neck, he didn't choke me though. "You'll regret feeling that way." He drug me out of the trailer by my neck and clenched his jaw. Before I could react to anything, he was doing he threw me down onto the grass. As soon as I landed the snakes slithered over to me. I tried to jump up and run but, they were faster. I felt a few bites but, I ignored the pain as I tried to crawl towards the gun.

Lewis walked in front of me, he stepped over me. I glanced up at him. He kicked the gun back. I grimaced as I felt another bite on my leg. I was feeling dizzy, I felt kind of sick to my stomach. I knew I wasn't going to be able to keep my eyes open much longer. Lewis was going to let me die, I was sure of that. I felt weak already. His body started to shrink; his skin started to turn a light tan color. I used my elbows to get to my knees. Lewis slowly transformed into a snake himself. I didn't have time to react to anything, I was dying. I couldn't believe what I was seeing but, I had more important things on my mind.

He hissed at me. I screamed at the size of the snake but, quickly rolled away from him. I was barely able to get to my knees. I used my knees as legs and wiggled towards the gun. My vision started getting fuzzy. I grabbed the gun and dropped onto my back. Lewis was above me; he had turned into an eight-foot snake. I ignored that and emptied my shotgun into Lewis. Even as a snake I could tell he was surprised. He didn't think I would ever really shoot him. He fell down. As his blood poured out onto the grass, he slowly turned back to a human.

Lewis's dead body laid at my feet. I dropped the gun as my strength faded. The snakes surrounded his body but, soon left him alone. I could feel my breathe getting shallow. The venom was taking over my body, killing me. It was okay because I knew Lewis was dead as well. Whatever he was couldn't hurt anybody else. I wondered what people would think happened here. The thought of the mystery I was leaving behind made me smile a little.

BOOK INSERT

CHAPTER 1:

THE LIFE I WANT

My name is Travis Edgewood, I'm a struggling writer. I wrote a romance novel that got me a little attention a few years ago but, sense then all the hype has died down immensely. Everything I had wrote sense then was basically ignored by my previous fans. This put me into a depression. I never leave my apartment; everything is delivered to me. I haven't left my apartment in four months; I don't mind it; I like being isolated. I play a lot of solitaire and chess to strengthen my mind. I've been living on cheap ramen and takeout for the longest time.

I pushed my reading glasses further onto my nose as I stared blankly at my computer screen. All I had down was a working title. I had no motivation to write. It's not like I didn't have ideas but, I just figured what was the point. Writing was hard to do when you no longer believed in your own talent. My name was all but forgotten in the writing community. I started off my writing career later in my life then I wanted. I popped my knuckles as I looked down at my keyboard. Writing always brought me such joy and I let my own brain ruin that. I stopped writing for fun and maybe my work reflected that. None of my friends wanted to hear about my depression anymore and I didn't really blame them. A knock on my door broke me out of my daze. I didn't think I had any packages coming but, it was hard to keep track.

I opened the door quickly wanting to get back to brainstorming. My heart skipped a beat at the sight of the doorman. He handed me a box "this was left at the desk." I grabbed it from him "thank you." He smiled and headed back down the hall. I watched him walk away. He was so handsome. Every time he talked to me, I just froze, I had a crush on him since the very first day I had moved in. We never talk, I don't think I could talk to him. He knew my name because of my packages but, I didn't even know his first name. I wasn't very good at love despite being a romance writer. I hadn't really ever had a relationship. Me and the doorman never even had a conversation I liked him solely on his looks, which I felt kind of guilty about. I didn't even know his ethnicity, I didn't care what he was but, it showed how little I knew about him.

I glanced back at my piano in the corner. I smiled "I bet I could impress him with my musical talents." I then blushed at my own embarrassment. I set the package down and opened it. It was just a book I had ordered. I removed my glasses and rubbed my eyes "come on Travis you have to write something today" I rolled my eyes. I really didn't want to write another story about someone else's happy ending when I couldn't even get a date.

Most of that was because I didn't leave my apartment but, I ignored that usually. I sat down at my desk and looked at the blank word document. Dread just fell on me as I lost all interest in starting my current novel. I opened a new word document. I couldn't stop thinking about the doorman, I wondered if he had read any of my books. I shook my head; he probably didn't even know I wrote books. I smiled "he looks like he might be a Nathaniel." I blushed "what a cute name." "If only I wasn't me...if I was stronger with my feelings, I wouldn't be so lost." For fun I started writing a short story. I decided to make it a futuristic western. I had a real passion for western movies so why not write one. I smiled as I started creating my western fusion setting. The world had gone back to the ways of the west but, modern technology still remained. I felt cheery as I started setting up my little story.

I hadn't written just for myself for a long while. "Maybe if I put in a self-insert." I always heard about people putting themselves into their stories to make it more of a fantasy for themselves. I never tried this form of writing, I thought it was tacky but, this story was for my own amusement so I decided to make myself the hero. I made myself the toughest man in the west, a man who never backed down from a dare or a fight. I chuckled as I wrote, I knew this was ridiculous but, it was enjoyable. I built up my personality, I made Travis Braveston a strong, brave man. Everything I wasn't. Since I was creating a fake version of my life, I decided to put Nathaniel in my story as well. No one was ever going to read this anyway. It was just a self-fanfiction. I quickly lost myself in my fake life to the point where I lost track of time. All I wanted to do was finish my story. I wished my life was as fun as Travis Braveston's. It wasn't long before I believed I was the person in my story.

Travis approached the saloon. It was golden hour; the sun was falling behind the trees. Travis entered the saloon; he searched the inside of the tavern looking for the outlaw Quickdraw, he had tracked him to this small town. He had passed through this town several times before so he knew most of the locals. He heard a familiar voice call to him. He turned to the bartender. "Mr. Braveston, that woman over there has requested time with you." He agreed to meet with the woman. She seemed nice enough, nothing about her stood out. She eyed Travis, looking at him with lustful intent. He sat down on the chair furthest away from her. "What can I do for you" he watched his surroundings as the woman started to speak. She smiled a little "well, Mr. Braveston I heard you never toss away a dare." This intrigued him. "Usually depends on the dare mam" he rubbed his chin. She looked at him with love in her eyes. Travis tried to ignore the lusty vibe he was getting from her. He knew he was a very handsome man, his muscular physique cut through his loose clothing.

He was used to this but, it kind of got on his nerves. The woman looked behind him as if she was looking for someone. He had been through something similar before. A woman was trying to help her sister or friends out. Travis denied her dare before he heard it. She gasped "all I was going to say was kiss the next person that enters the saloon." He rolled his eyes "sorry mam but, I'm not kissing anybody." Travis stood up and turned. He was stopped in his tracks as a stranger he never saw before entered the saloon. He saw a young girl coming in behind him. He figured this must be the girl that the woman was trying to help out. He focused on the man; he was kind of weak looking. His handsome face overshadowed his dirty clothing. Travis smirked "I think I will take that dare."

Travis was astounded by his face; he had never seen such a beautiful person. The man walked over to the bar and sat down. Travis ignored the pleas of the woman as her friend walked towards him. He was fixated on him. He leaned on the bar next to the man. He looked nervous as Travis leaned near him. "What's the name?" "Nathaniel" his voice was softer than he thought it would be. Travis blushed when he mentioned his name "that's an adorable name." Nathaniel seemed confused "did I do something?" "No but, I was dared to do something...don't be afraid." "I'm Travis Braveston by the way." Nathaniel shook his head "okay, well what was the dare?" He seemed more afraid than anything. Travis got closer to him. Nathaniel leaned away from him "what are you doing?" He leaned and gently grabbed his wrist "I was dared to kiss you." Nathaniel gulped "me...why?" Travis held his wrist gently "I've never turned down a dare...especially one as rewarding as this."

He could tell Nathaniel was nervous. He wrapped his other arm around Nathaniel's back to secure him. He noticed how flushed Nathaniel had gotten from his simple touches. Travis rubbed his back with his hand "come on you don't want to ruin my reputation, do you?" "Umm, no I guess but, I've never..." Travis leaned in and pushed Nathaniel to him. Travis took his hand off his wrist and put it on his chin. Travis knelt down and kissed his lips. He could feel him shaking under his lips. Travis pulled away slowly so that Nathaniel wouldn't react. His face was red, he cupped his mouth with his hand. "Are you embarrassed" Travis asked? He shook his head "a little, I didn't know you meant in front of everyone."

A loud knock on my door took me out of the story, I rubbed my eyes "I wrote thirty thousand words." I yawned, I wanted to get back to the story but, whoever knocked wouldn't stop knocking. I noticed my chest was hurting a little but I ignored it and got up. My legs were so stiff, I almost couldn't walk on them. I made my way to the door. I opened it quickly wanting them to leave so I could finish my story. I leaned back and blushed "Nathaniel." He looked at me strangely "who?" I shook my head and tried not to look into his eyes "nothing, I'm just a little tired." I opened the door and stepped towards him "what can I do for you?" Just being near him made my heart skip beats, I know I hadn't really kissed him but, I still felt as if we had gained a moment together.

I adjusted my glasses as he started talking to me. "Nothing crazy but, the building is going to be under construction next month, I just wanted to let everyone know about the noise." I couldn't help but, stare at his jawline. It looked like it would cut me if I touched it. I hid my shaking hands "okay thank you." He started walking to the next apartment, I closed my door. "Seriously I still couldn't ask him his name!" I ran back to my computer. "I can be brave enough in my own story...I control everything." My throat was scratchy and my mouth was out of spit. I knew a few hours had gone by but, I sat down and started my story again. I wasn't sure how long it had been because I was so focused but, I felt as if

I had typed for two days straight. My short story had turned into a novel. I couldn't stop myself from writing down my thoughts about Nathaniel. Maybe if I completed the story, I would have more confidence in my writing and in my personal life. I rubbed my eyes before focusing back on the words in front of me.

Travis knew that Quickdraw had taken Nathaniel away in the night. He knew their paths would cross until one of them was killed. Quickdraw had left a note wrapped around what appeared to be a chunk of Nathaniel's dark hair. Travis was prepared to die if he had to but, he had to save his boyfriends life. It was almost pitch black outside the moon barely lit the trail as he walked towards the remains of a drive-in theater. He had his finger on the trigger, Quickdraw would most likely shoot as soon as he saw Travis. He tried to look at everything he could with every step.

I grabbed my chest as a sharp pain went through my heart, it quickly passed but, it took me out of my concentration. I looked at my phone, I had been writing for another four hours. Time really flies when your focused on another world. My throat hurt a little from dryness. I managed to almost complete an entire book in a few days, I was very impressed with myself. "I just needed to finish the final confrontation between Quickdraw and me...I mean Travis." I chuckled "well he is kind of me." I turned to the window "how many times has the sun risen since I've been sitting here?" I quickly threw the question behind me and tried finishing my climax. It was odd that I wasn't sleepy, I figured it was because I was so intrigued with my own story.

Travis backed up against the rusted remains of what he assumed was an old car. It was a windy night. He calmed his breathing if he lost focus Nathaniel would surely be killed. The only building in the field was what remained of the snack booth. "He has to be there" he whispered to himself. Travis tried to stay to the shadows as he walked towards the small building. He hoped Nathaniel was okay, if he was hurt because of his involvement with outlaws, he could never forgive himself. He didn't really have the right to act like he was the law but, the rush from it was what Travis often craved. He was worried for Nathaniel but, he couldn't help but, feel some sense of heroism as he approached the building. He was going to save the person closest to him it was going to be a big moment for their relationship. Would Nathaniel be grateful or upset.

Travis put his back to the brick wall. He tried to listen for voices but, he heard nothing. A thought went through his mind, he had to put his hand against the wall so he wouldn't lose his balance "what if he killed him already." He pushed the troublesome thought from his mind. He put his finger on the trigger of his pistol. He leapt away from the wall and ran inside of the open door. The room was darker than it looked. He knew it was stupid to run in without being able to see but, he couldn't take not knowing how Nathaniel was doing. Travis looked around; his eyes slowly adjusted to the scenery around him. He didn't see anyone or any objects resembling a human being.

I felt pressure in my chest and immediately stopped writing. I grabbed at my chest as the pain became so unbearable, I fell out of my chair. I clutched my chest with my hands. Was I having a heart attack? Maybe I pushed myself to hard. My phone was on my desk but, I couldn't get up off of the ground. The pain was too much, I hadn't noticed how tired I was before. I was so excited about my writing for once in such a long time that I had forgotten what it felt like. I could feel my eyes start to pool with tears. I didn't want to lose that feeling. So, this is how Travis Edgewood dies, I thought. Curled up in a ball writing a self-insert. All of the depression I had felt over the past years was finally ending. "I just wanted to make myself happy." I felt the tears roll down my cheeks "I never got to save Nathaniel."

EMPTY

CHAPTER 1:

THE NEW GIRL

I sat down in my desk, ready for whatever science nonsense I wasn't going to understand for the day. I hated physics; it was the worse class of the day because I didn't have any friends in it. I didn't have many friends as it is, being alone in a class for forty-five minutes reminded me of that. I pulled out a pen and waited for class to start, I wasn't very smart but, I tried to be a good student. I watched the clock tick away for what seemed like forever. I didn't bounce out of the trance until I felt the desk next to me shake. It only startled me because nobody sat near me. A girl I had never seen before sat down next to me. I didn't like stereotyping people but, she dressed kind of artsy. She was in the middle of speed texting. She noticed I was looking at her "hi." She lightly waved "is it okay if the new girl sits with you?" I was a little shocked at how outspoken she sounded "umm, yeah nobody sits there."

She smiled "names Rena, what's yours?" "Emberly Bates" I felt weird for saying my last name." She seemed to think it was funny. Rena picked up her phone and started speed texting again "sorry but, I'm trying to get my ex to take me back." I shook my hands "oh I didn't mean to stare!" She shrugged "yeah I know, I just thought I should tell you."

I thought about how weird it was for her to tell me something so personal but, I ignored it. Rena kept texting all throughout class, I was surprised no one noticed. I saw her sneak vitamins a few times. I wondered if she was sick. We had two more classes together. It was kind of nice to have someone to talk to. After school we walked out together. I was really the only person who tried talking to Rena, at least what I saw. Everyone seemed to be ignoring her.

She rolled her eyes as we walked outside "seriously." She stared out into the rain "I have to walk home." I smirked "so do I, I live close by...we can run there." I shrugged "if you want, I know you don't know me all that well." Rena didn't think about it at all she just answered "yeah!" She rolled up her sleeves "how far?" "one block" I pointed. We took off running, I felt kind of weird letting a stranger into my apartment but, I was very low on friends so it seemed like the right thing to do. Rena followed me into my apartment. She looked around "doesn't look that big for a family?" I had already gotten used to how outspoken she was. "It's only me...my parents pay for me to live near the school, everything's in walking distance for me." Rena laughed "what parents can afford to do that, you're still in high school?" "Well I don't know if you noticed around the city but, the name Bates is kind of everywhere." Rena set her bag down "oh I thought I remembered seeing that name on the hospital this morning." I took off my flannel shirt "are you hungry?" She smiled softly "no" she pointed to me "so if you're like the city rich girl...how am I your only friend?" I honestly didn't know why this was so I gave her my reasoning instead. "I just don't click with a lot of people I guess."

"Emberly I tell you this because I think we're becoming friends...never where a flannel and a band t-shirt to school ever again." I laughed "will do." We watched *Netflix* for a few hours as we waited for the rain to stop. I used my parents credit card to order take out. I noticed she took several more pills throughout the evening. I wanted to ask her if she was sick but, I couldn't bring myself to ask. She texted her ex a lot, the person must be that special, I thought. We talked all evening but, I still didn't learn much about her. I fell asleep a little after dinner.

I felt cold, I rubbed my shoulders until I eventually opened my eyes. I was looking right at the ceiling. As my eyes fully opened, I started to realize the pain

I was in. My entire body hurt; I was on the floor in my living room. It wasn't a slight pain; the pain was so bad I wanted to cry. I touched my stomach, most of the pain was centered there. I flinched as I ran my hand over my stomach. I didn't appear to be bleeding. I rolled onto my stomach, I held in my screams as I got to my knees. I felt like I could barely stand up.

What had happened to me? I slowly made my way to the bathroom, every step feeling like a mile. I barely had the strength to flick the light on. I checked my body in the mirror looking for bruises and cuts but, I saw nothing. I felt like I needed to puke. I never felt so bad in my life. I wondered if I had some extreme case of food poising. Maybe Rena had it to? I thankfully had my phone in my pocket, I called 911. I really didn't think I could walk back on my own. I felt as if I might pass out at any time. I leaned against the mirror until the paramedics showed up.

I was kind of out of it for most of the procedures. However, even when I awoke later on the next day, I was still in so much pain I couldn't move. My parents had stopped by to ask me questions about the incident only I didn't know what to tell them. I felt so weak that talking took a lot of my energy. It wasn't long before the doctors figured out what was wrong with me. An MRI basically confirmed what was wrong with me within the first hour but, I wasn't able to wake up for that. They learned that half of every organ in my body had been halved, right down the middle. No cuts, it was so clean everyone said the only way it could have happened was by magic. That's not something you usually hear in a hospital.

I now had half a heart, one lung and one kidney...and so on. I wasn't born this way because I had had plenty of MRI scans in my life, something had happened recently. I couldn't prove it but, I knew it was Rena. I never could prove it because no one ever heard of her. I told the police I didn't know her last name but, she was in a lot of my classes. The thing was that nobody with that name was registered at the school, none of the students remembered seeing her that day. I knew I wasn't crazy because now I was bedridden because of my weakened state. Rena had destroyed my life in one day, I was too desperate for friends I guess but, normal people wouldn't worry about losing half of their organs. Everyone tells me Rena doesn't exist but, I talked to her all day, she came to my house. There is no other explanation for my current state.

Somewhere out there I know Rena was running around charming people into trusting her, I don't know what she's doing with my organs but, they're not a part of me anymore.

RED WOLF

CHAPTER 1:

THE ASYLUM

The room was dark, it smelled of rubbing alcohol and cleaning supplies. It was quieter than she thought it would be. She pulled back her arms as she tried to escape the restraints. She was still dizzy from whatever they had given her. "Selene!" She knew she could hear her name being called but, she couldn't bring herself to speak. Four full grown men were trying to tie her down to the bed. The nurse had to step in for assistance.

Selene felt a needle pierce her skin. She flinched at the sudden burning she felt. The pain was intense "please...metal can kill me" she barely mumbled before she blacked out. The nurse ignored her comment and continued restraining her. The four guys relaxed once Selene was strapped to the bed. One of the guys popped his arm "for a small girl she's extremely strong." The nurse wrote down what she had witnessed.

After the men left, Nurse Abby opened up the windows. She knew seeing the sunlight might ease Selene's mind. She looked over her paperwork on her new patient. Most of it she had already figured out for herself. Selene Benson was often violent and had schizophrenia and paranoia. Abby leaned over the bed and glanced over Selene's body. She noticed her dark skin was covered in small burn marks where the metal restraint bracelets had been. She looked at her arm, her skin was freshly burned from where she had just given her the shot. She franticly looked over her paperwork, she saw nothing about a metal allergy. "Maybe it's not metals maybe she's allergic to nickel?"

She wondered if it was a mistake in the paperwork. She left the room to call the doctor that had sent her to the asylum. As soon as the door closed Selene's eyes shot open, she panicked as she searched the room. She looked down at the restraints. "Where am I" she muttered to herself. The last thing she remembered was a man asking her last name before pulling her into his car. She found it strange how he was able to overpower her. Usually no mortal man could ever lay a finger on her. She shrugged it off as he obviously was like her, or something like her.

She knew she wasn't out for long, most drugs had little to no effect on her. She felt dizzy still, she wondered how much drugs they had pumped into her to get her to fall asleep. Selene made a fist as she tried to pull off the restraint straps. She knew she could but, she was in such a weak condition she stopped herself. She wanted to save her strength. The room was small, she looked out the window, the sun was starting to set. Her hands started shaking, she didn't know what day it was. She could hear the sounds of footsteps approaching. The door slowly opened. "Please you have to let me out of here..." Abby interrupted her by gasping "how are you awake, you should've been out for at least forty-five minutes.

Selene shook her head "what day is it?" She set down a plate of food "it's Wednesday." She noticed the fear that soon covered her face "Selene do you have an allergy to metal or something because I noticed..." She cut her off "look miss" she looked at her nametag "Abby, you need to let me out of here now or everyone in this hospital will die tonight!" Abby frowned "that's not funny in the slightest" she picked up a sandwich "please eat something." She hovered the sandwich near her lips "Selene please." She bit into the sandwich and started gulping it down, she was starved, she always was.

She quickly ate the remainder of her meal. Selene looked Abby up and down, she seemed nice. She swallowed hard as Abby gave her the last bite of her dinner. "Are you thirsty?" She shook her head as she looked out the window "no but, I'd like to get up and walk around, my legs are numb." Abby shook her head "I would like to do that but, I can't...maybe we can go for a walk outside tomorrow morning." "No" she yelled "it will be too late, please believe me...you need to let me go!"

"I read your chart Selene I know all of your habits, I'm sorry but, it's not happening!" She grunted loudly "look I am not human, when the full moon is in the sky tonight, I won't be able to control myself!" Abby shrugged her shoulders jokingly "what are you telling me you're a werewolf or something?" Selene bit her lip for a second, thinking over her next words carefully "yes, I am a werewolf from the Benson line." Her voice got lower "I know how stupid it sounds but, in a few hours, I won't be able to control myself, I could transform right now and escape but, I want to use my energy to try and hold off my urges until I'm far away from civilization."

She knew the nurse didn't believe a word she was saying. She didn't really blame her she knew she sounded like she was out of her mind. "Anything you've read about me in those papers wasn't true, I have no medical problems...something else is going on." Selene knew her pure blood made her a target but, she kept that to herself. Most werewolves were watered down versions of pure blood werewolves but, Selene's power could easily take out any normal werewolf. Without realizing it she had made a fist, the irritation in her voice distracted Abby from looking down. She knew as the night neared; she would gradually get stronger. "Let me out now!" Her anger got the best of her and she pulled up her arm. The metal restraint bend like plastic. "Abby we only have a few hours come on, please!"

Abby walked towards the door "apparently we need some stronger medication to knock you out for the night." She shook her head "nothing you have will keep the wolf from coming out" she looked down at the bent metal "you don't leave me a choice." Abby quickly left, most likely to get help from other faculty. Selene knew she didn't have much of a chance, with all the drugs they had pumped into her over the last few hours. She was weakened but, she was still stronger than the average human.

She flexed her muscles and pulled her arms upwards. The feeling of the metal touching her burned her skin, she put the pain out her mind as she continued flexing her body up. The metal slowly starting to bend over. Selene let out a scream as she used her body to push her upper body forward. The metal bent out enough that she could easily slip out. She hit the floor, as her eyesight started to get fuzzy again. She rubbed her eyes, if she turned into a wolf, she could jump through the window. She knew she could make a clean break for it but, she feared if she'd be able to control herself so close to the full moon. "It doesn't matter" she mumbled. She used the bed to stabilize her numb legs. She took a deep breathe. She went towards the window, it had bars on it. She knew she could bend them with time. She punched through the glass because she noticed the window had an electronic alarm on top of them. She knew if she opened the window normally, she would alert the whole hospital of her escape.

Her hand stung a little from the glass but, she wasn't too worried about it. Blood dripped all over the window as she reached through the window and grabbed one of the bars. She pulled on it with all her might until she felt it crumble in her hand. The bars were a little rusty, which only helped her. She could hear fast approaching footsteps. She crumbled a second bar before she heard the sound of the door slamming open.

Selene jerked away from the window, she looked back at the door wondering how many people she was going to have to fight off. To her surprise it was just Abby. She knew she heard lots of footsteps, she assumed they were waiting outside of the room. "Ms. Benson please get away from that window" she tried to hide how shocked she was "you're bleeding." "Trust me I will be fine; you need to leave me alone!" "Abby you are just doing your job but, I am trying to stop myself from literally tearing you apart" she hated to be so vulgar but, she didn't know how else to get her attention.

Abby was hiding her hands behind her back, most likely holding a syringe full of something that was going to knock her out. Selene rubbed her eyes "Abby, I don't want to hurt you." The nurse tightened up her arms "Selene you aren't going to hurt anyone, we'll help you with your delusions." The room was silent. Selene could clearly hear the men tightening restraints in the hallway. She knew she had little chance of removing the rest of the bars before they all came in and stopped her. She knew she could easily get past the nurse. Selene straightened up her back and faced the doorway, Abby was standing in the way but, she knew she was plenty fast.

Selene took off and ran towards Abby. She didn't expect this because she jumped out of the way. Selene ran past her with ease, once at the door she ran through knowing there were men on the other side. She didn't really care; she knew she would be out in a few hours anyway if her wolf personality took over. She still wanted to have as little human causalities as she could. As soon as she entered the hallway one man tried to wrap his arms around her as a form of restraint. Selene pushed him off easily with her elbow. She put a little force behind it but she wasn't really sure if she overdid it or not.

She didn't bother to check. She noticed seven men surrounding her. The hallway was rather large. She elbowed one man in the jaw as she tried to run through the group of men. They all seemed shocked at her strength. Two of the men tried to hold her down while the others tried to restrain her. She heard Abby's slight yelp. Selene started walking as they tried to hold her down, she slowly pulled them along with her as she walked down the hallway. She felt something metal pierce her skin. It was Abby giving her a shot. She ignored the dizziness and kept walking.

Another man grabbed ahold of her arm and violently pulled her back. She felt a slight pain in her arm as the man tried to pull her to the ground. She pulled against him with such force that it knocked him down. Selene jerked as she felt a sharp pain in her shoulder. It must be another shot she thought to herself. She dropped down to her hands and knees; she had no choice she had to transform in front of them. If she didn't, they would all die later. She knew they were only doing their jobs. They didn't deserve to die because of that. Once she knelt down, they started tying her down. She felt another injection. Before she could transform into her wolf form her vision went black. She felt her body hit the floor.

A few hours later her eyes opened, upon opening her eyes she already knew what had happened. The smell of blood was overwhelming. She was cold, she looked down at her naked body and immediately knew she had transformed. Her skin was covered in blood. The metallic taste was creeping onto her taste buds. Her eyes searched the room she was in. She didn't really recognize it but, it looked like a lobby. The room was completely dark but, she could easily see. She sighed as she saw two bodies in the hallway that had literally been ripped apart.

Selene started searching for clothing that wasn't blood stained. She wasn't worried, sadly she knew there weren't any people left alive in the building. All she could smell was death. She felt immense regret however, she had been through this so many times that she had grown somewhat cold to it. Selene walked through the hospital until she found a breakroom. She rummaged through all the lockers until she found an oversized green hoodie. As she slipped it on, she noticed the body of a nurse slumped up against the wall. She sniffed the air, even amongst all the blood in the room she could still smell Abby.

She knelt down by her to see how much damage she had caused to Abby's face. Luckily it was still intact. She had scribbled something on her notepad. Selene only looked because she saw the word wolf. She read the panicked writings. *It was a wolf, a wolf red with blood, Selene Benson is a wolf!* She didn't bother taking the paper. She was a pureblood werewolf no normal human could ever truly harm her. She was more worried about who put her in the asylum in the first place. Purebloods were only targeted for two reasons, for breeding or the blood curse. She wondered if it could be something tabooer like vampire involvement. She shook her head; she didn't really want to concern herself with the issues of her entrapment. She walked right through the front door and into the surrounding forests. With only the full moons light to guide her.

AUTHOR NOTES

The short story *Red Wolf* will become the first introduction in an upcoming series for the future. Ever since I started writing I wanted to do a vampire series and build a book universe around it. The introduction of this storyline is a promise to eventually build a book universe around vampires and werewolves. I have three book universes I want to build upon, one of them being the *Elemental Mystics* universe which has already been established with *Bond's in Time*.

THANK YOU FOR
THE READ

Printed in the USA
CPSIA information can be obtained
at www.ICGtesting.com
LVHW040350061023
760079LV00015B/531